D0405623

Bo and the Community Garden

by Elliott Smith
illustrated by Subi Bosa

Cicely Lewis, Executive Editor

Lerner Publications ◆ Minneapolis

A Letter from Cicely Lewis

Dear Reader,
　This series is about a boy named Bo and his grandfather in the barbershop called the Buzz. The barbershop has always been the hub of the Black community. In a world  where Black voices are often silenced, it is a place where these voices can be heard.
　I created the Read Woke challenge for my students so they can read books that reflect the diversity of the world. I hope you see the real-life beauty, richness, and joy of Black culture shine through these pages.
　　　　　　—Cicely Lewis, Executive Editor

TABLE OF CONTENTS

Bo's World

Hi, I'm Bo. I like basketball,
science, and flying in airplanes.
This is my grandpa, Roger.
I call him Pop-Pop.

We live upstairs from the Buzz. It's the barbershop Pop-Pop owns.

I like hanging out with my friends Silas, Shawn, and Zuri.

CHAPTER 1

An Opportunity

6

Bo and Shawn were in a heated game of paper soccer before class. *Flick!* Bo's goal sailed through Shawn's fingers. "I win!" Bo shouted just as the bell rang.

Ms. Williams walked into class with a guest. Zuri poked Bo and whispered, "Who's that?" Bo shrugged.

"Good morning, class," Ms. Williams said. "This is Mrs. Chu. She teaches fifth grade. She's here to announce a new project."

"Hi everyone," Mrs. Chu said. "Our school is starting a community garden. Your class will be assigned spots in it. You'll get to grow whatever you like."

"Awesome!" Bo said.

"Each group of four students will get their own plot," Ms. Williams said. "Now, let's all go out to the garden and explore!"

Bo, Silas, Zuri, and Shawn decided to be a group. When they went to see the garden, they all had their own ideas.

"We should grow a cactus," Shawn said.

Zuri shook her head. "No way! Sunflowers."

11

Silas scrunched his nose. "How about a spider plant?" he said.

"That's silly," Bo said. "We should plant an orange tree!"

Bo and his friends argued the whole time they were at the garden. They were all upset when they went back to class. And they had no idea what to plant.

CHAPTER 2
Planting Seeds

Bo cleaned a mirror at the Buzz. He was still frustrated with his friends. He didn't know how they would ever agree on what to plant.

"Pop-Pop, have you ever had a garden?" he asked.

Bo's grandpa looked up from cutting a man's hair. "No, I'm not really used to growing things. I'm better at cutting," he said with a wink.

"We can't figure out what to grow in our school garden spot," Bo said sadly.

"I have an idea," said the man in the chair. "I work at the homeless shelter. We always try to give healthy food to people who need help. Fresh vegetables are a big deal."

"Mr. Darren is right," Pop-Pop said. He got a dreamy look on his face. "You know what sounds good? Some okra. Your ancestors brought that plant all the way from Africa!"

"I don't really like vegetables," Bo said. "But if we can help people, that would be good."

Mr. Darren laughed. "Maybe you'll love the vegetables you grow. We'd be so happy to have them at the shelter."

Bo ran upstairs. He wanted to read about the best vegetables to grow. He was excited to tell his friends about the new plan.

CHAPTER 3
Green Thumbs

Bo and his friends gathered at the playground at recess. Everyone apologized for their argument. Then Bo shared Mr. Darren's idea of growing vegetables for the shelter. "What do you think?" he asked.

"That sounds great," Zuri said. "My mom volunteers there. She'll be so happy!"

The friends ran over to the garden. They found Mrs. Chu digging in the dirt. Bo told her their idea.

"I love it," she said. "I'll get the seeds you need so you can start planting on Monday."

On Monday, Bo's class went back to the garden. Bo pulled on his bright yellow gardening gloves. Mrs. Chu helped Bo and his friends get started. She brought tomato cages and seeds to grow tomatoes, okra, and lettuce.

Bo and Shawn dug holes using garden trowels. Zuri carefully planted the seeds in a row. Silas watered the covered seeds.

"Tomatoes and okra are a good pair," Mrs. Chu said. "The tomato plants help keep harmful bugs away from the okra. They'll both grow nicely if you care for them."

"I can't wait to try them," Bo said. "And I can't wait to bring them to the shelter!"

"These vegetables will help a lot of people," Mrs. Chu said.

Bo smiled. It felt nice to do something for others.

About the Author

Elliott Smith has been writing stories ever since he was a kid. This love of writing led him first to a career as a sports reporter. Now, he has written more than 40 children's books, both fiction and nonfiction. Smith lives just outside Washington, DC, with his wife and two children. He loves watching movies, playing basketball with his kids, and adding to his collection of Pittsburgh Steelers memorabilia.

About the Illustrator

As a child, Subi Bosa drew pictures all the time, in every room of the house—sometimes on the walls. His mother still tells everyone, "He knew how to draw before he could properly hold a pencil." In 2020, Subi was awarded a Mo Siewcharran Prize for Illustration. Subi lives in Cape Town, South Africa, creating picture books, comics, and graphic novels.

Lerner Publications Company
An imprint of Lerner Publishing Group, Inc.
241 First Avenue North
Minneapolis, MN 55401 USA

For reading levels and more information, look up this title at www.lernerbooks.com.

Main body text set in Mikado 24/41. Typeface provided by Hannes von Doehren.

Library of Congress Cataloging-in-Publication Data

Names: Smith, Elliott, 1976– author. | Bosa, Subi, illustrator.
Title: Bo and the community garden / by Elliott Smith ; illustrated by Subi Bosa.
Description: Minneapolis : Lerner Publications, [2023] | Series: Bo at the Buzz (Read woke chapter books) | Audience: Ages 6-9. | Audience: Grades 2-3. | Summary: Bo and his friends cannot agree on what to plant in their plot at the school community garden.
Identifiers: LCCN 2022014270 (print) | LCCN 2022014271 (ebook) | ISBN 9781728476179 (lib. bdg.) | ISBN 9781728486314 (pbk.) | ISBN 9781728481395 (eb pdf)
Subjects: CYAC: Gardening—Fiction. | African Americans—Fiction. | LCGFT: Fiction.
Classification: LCC PZ7.1.S626 Boc 2023 (print) | LCC PZ7.1.S626 (ebook) | DDC [Fic]—dc23

LC record available at https://lccn.loc.gov/2022014270
LC ebook record available at https://lccn.loc.gov/2022014271

Manufactured in the United States of America
1 – CG – 12/15/22